A NOTE TO PARENTS

Early Step into Reading Books are designed for preschoolers and kindergartners who are just getting ready to read. The words are easy, the type is big, and the stories are packed with rhyme, rhythm, and repetition.

We suggest that you read this book to your child the first few times, pointing to each word as you go. Soon your child will start saying the words with you. And before long, he or she will try to read the story alone. Don't be surprised if your child uses the pictures to figure out the text—that's what they're there for! The important thing is to develop your child's confidence—and to show your child that reading is fun.

When your child is ready to move on, try the rest of the steps in our Step into Reading series. **Step 1 Books** (preschool–grade 1) feature the same easy-to-read type as the Early Step into Reading Books, but with more words per page. **Step 2 Books** (grades 1–3) are both longer and slightly more difficult, while **Step 3 Books** (grades 2–3) introduce readers to paragraphs and fully developed plot lines. **Step 4 Books** (grades 2–4) offer exciting nonfiction for the increasingly independent reader.

The grade levels assigned to the five steps are intended only as guides. Some children move through all five steps very rapidly; others climb the steps over a period of several years. Either way, these books will help your child "step into reading" in style!

Copyright © 1991 by Richard Scarry.
All rights reserved under International and Pan-American Copyright Conventions. Published in the United States by Random House, Inc., New York, and simultaneously in Canada by Random House of Canada Limited, Toronto. Originally published in a slightly different form in 1991 as a Random House Pictureback® Reader. First Random House Early Step into Reading™ edition, 1997.

http://www.randomhouse.com/

Library of Congress Cataloging-in-Publication Data
Scarry, Richard. Watch your step, Mr. Rabbit! / by Richard Scarry.
p. cm. — (Early step into reading) SUMMARY: Mr. Rabbit's feet get stuck in the street as he looks at his newspaper.
ISBN 0-679-88650-8 (trade) — ISBN 0-679-98650-2 (lib. bdg.) [1. Rabbits—Fiction.]
I. Title. II. Series. PZ7.S327Wat 1997 [E]—dc21 96-47712

Printed in the United States of America 10 9 8 7 6 5 4 3 2 1

STEP INTO READING is a registered trademark of Random House, Inc.

Early Step into Reading™

Richard Scarry's
Watch Your Step, Mr. Rabbit!

Random House 🏠 New York

Here comes Mr. Rabbit.

Is he looking

at his feet?

7

No.

He is looking
at his newspaper.

Now he is looking
at his feet.
His feet are stuck
in the street.

Can we push him out?

No!

13

Can we pull him out?

No!

Can we blow him out?

16

No!

17

Can we squirt him out?

No, we cannot!

His feet are
good and stuck.

Aha!

We can scoop him out!

Mr. Rabbit

is not stuck now.

There goes Mr. Rabbit.

He is looking

at his newspaper again.

Oh, no!

Watch your step,
Mr. Rabbit!